專門替中國人寫的英文課本

中級本（上冊）

從蜻蜓點水到小題大做

李家同

這兩本書是《專門替中國人寫的英文課本》的中級本，比起初級本來，這兩本當然高級多了，至少讀了這兩本書以後，我們可以學會如何使用現在完成式、過去完成式、過去進行式、被動語氣以及其他相當重要的英文基本規則。

就以現在完成式為例，我曾經看過目前很多國中英文教科書如何介紹這種觀念的，他們的介紹方法很簡單，在一篇文章中間，有很多很多的句子用的都是現在完成式，然後在文章的後面，會有一兩個例子，介紹過去分詞 (past participle)，也介紹一下現在完成式的定義，這一下就大功告成矣。

什麼情況之下，要用現在完成式，這些教科書無法解釋，這些書的作者當然知道什麼情況之下要用現在完成式，但是他們不能在英文教科書裡用中文解釋觀念，當然又不能用英文解釋，因為畢竟這些書都是寫給小孩子看的，你用英文解釋現在完成式的用法，誰看得懂呢？

這本書的最大優點，就是在於它痛痛快快地用中文解釋英文的基本規則，我一直在想，如果不這樣做，如何能教好英文？英文不是那麼簡單的，我敢說，很多人一輩子弄不清楚現在式的意義，我們其實是不能輕易用現在式的，可是我們卻會不停地犯錯，濫用現在式。為什麼？還不是因為我們沒有在入門的英文教科書中將現在式解釋清楚。

大多數的英文教科書，因為不能用中文解釋，對於任何英文的基本規

則，都只好蜻蜓點水一樣地輕輕帶過，有些重要的議題，甚至在書中一字不提，難怪我國很多學生到了大學，寫英文句子仍然是錯誤百出。

這本書的作風正好相反，作者對於每一個英文規則，都詳加解釋，以人稱代名詞的受格而言，就整整講了一課，如果一位同學忽然之間對於這方面弄不清楚了，可以翻到這一課來，我們可以保證他一定會找到所要的資料。

讀英文，就要勤加練習，這本書的另一優點是練習題奇多，任何同學做了這麼多的練習題，當然都會對這些規則很熟悉了。

但是，學英文，總會犯錯的，所以這本書就設計了很多改錯的練習題。大家千萬不要小看了這些改錯習題，很多大學生進了研究所，甚至已經是博士班學生了，仍然在犯這些錯。如果這些大學生當年做過這類改錯的題目，情形一定會好得多。

這兩本書裡仍有中翻英的練習題，這是十分值得讚揚的。我們初學英文，不可能一開始就想英文句子的，我們當然會從中文句子想起，所以練習中翻英是有其必要的。最重要的是，一旦學生會將很多中文句子翻成英文，他的信心一定會大增，因為他會有相當好的成就感。舉例來說，如果你請學生翻譯「我從未去過台南。」，他脫口而出 "I have never been to Tainan."，試問他會多快樂。

這兩本書裡有整段的文章出現，有趣的是，這些文章都有解釋的，這恐怕也是創舉，我沒有看到別的英文教科書有這種做法。

目次

第一課

人稱代名詞

（受格）

　　我們常說給了某人東西，例如：I gave Amy a book.，或喜歡某本書，例如：I like this book.這些接受我們東西的人(Amy)，或被我們喜歡的物品(this book)，都可以用「人稱代名詞的受格」來取代，使句子更簡潔。

　　例如：I gave Amy a book. → I gave her a book.

　　　　　I like this book. → I like it.

1-1 生字

grandfather	祖父 簡稱為 grandpa
grandmother	祖母 簡稱為 grandma
parents	父母
grandparents	祖父母
give	給（give, gave）
a lot	非常
girl	女孩
toy car	玩具汽車
pencil	鉛筆
for	為了（介系詞）
birthday	生日

1-2 課文

My grandma gave me a toy car for my birthday.

我的祖母為了我的生日給了我一部玩具汽車。

I like it a lot.

我非常喜歡它。

My grandpa calls his friends every day.

我的祖父每天都打電話給他的朋友。

He likes to call them.

他喜歡打電話給他們。

My parents gave my sister and me many books yesterday.

昨天我的父母給我的姊姊和我很多書。

They gave us a lot of good books.

他們給了我們很多好書。

Does he like his English teacher Ms. Lin?

他喜歡他的英文老師——林女士嗎？（Mr. Lin林先生，Ms. Lin林女士）

Yes, he does. He likes her very much.

是的。他很喜歡她。

What did your grandparents give you last night?

你的祖父母昨晚給你什麼東西？

They gave me ten pencils.

他們給我 10 枝鉛筆。

 1-2-1 圖表

主格	所有格	受格
I 我	my 我的	me （給）我
you 你	your 你的	you 你
he 他	his 他的	him 他
she 她	her 她的	her 她
it 它、牠	its 牠的、它的	it 它、牠
we 我們	our 我們的	us 我們
you 你們	your 你們的	you 你們
they 他們	their 他們的	them 他們

My grandma	gave	me	a toy car	yesterday.
Your grandma	gave	you	a toy car,	too.
My parents	called	my aunt (her)		last week.
My English teacher	gave	the dog (it)	a ball	last month.
Tom	likes	his friends (them)	very much.	
Amy	gave	my brother and me (us)	two pencils.	
Amy	gave	you and your sister (you)	two pencils,	too.

注意：give（給），call（打電話）都是發生過的事情，要用過去式。

　　like（喜歡）某人是個事實，要用現在式來描述。

1-3-1 填填人稱代名詞受格：

1. I like my sisters.

   → I like _____.

2. I didn't like this movie at all.

   → I didn't like _____ at all.

3. She called her sister last night.

   → She called _____ last night.

4. The teacher gave my friend and me ten pencils.

   → The teacher gave _____ ten pencils.

5. He loves his grandfather very much.

   → He loves _____ very much.

6. My dad saw you and your brother in the park yesterday.

   → He saw _____ yesterday.

7. Amy called your sister today.

   → She called _____ today.

8. My mother gave my brother a toy car for his birthday.

   → She gave _____ a toy car for his birfhady.

9. She writes her parents a letter every day.

   → She writes _____ a letter every day.

10. My grandparents read 10 books every month.

    → They read _____ every month.

11. His mom likes this computer game very much.

→ She likes _____ very much.

12. My dad likes his students a lot.

→ He likes _____ a lot.

13. Who gave you this pencil?

→ My parents gave _____ to me.

14. Do you want to watch TV now?

→ No, I don't want to watch _____.

15. Did you call your parents last night?

→ No, I didn't call _____ last night.

16. Did you read this book last night?

→ Yes, I did. I read _____ last night.

17. When did you do your homework?

→ I did _____ last night.

18. Who ate this cake in the afternoon?

→ Ms. Lin ate _____ in the afternoon.

19. When do you watch TV?

→ I watch _____ every night.

20. How do you like Mr. Lin's book?

→ I like _____ very much.

1-3-2 英文該如何說？

1. Do you like English?

是的，我非常喜歡它。

_____ very much.

2.　What did your aunt give you for your birthday?

　　她給我一輛腳踏車（bike）。

　　_____

3.　Did your teacher call you last night?

　　是的，她昨晚打電話給我。

　　_____

4.　Can you see Amy?

　　是的，我可以看到她。

　　_____

5.　Where did you see my brother yesterday?

　　我在學校（at school）看到他。

　　_____

　　（＊see 的過去式是 saw）

6.　Does your mom like computer games?

　　是的，她喜歡它們。

　　_____

7.　Did Amy give you and your brother some pencils?

　　是的，她給了我們鉛筆。

　　_____

8.　What do you call your dog?

　　我叫（call）牠 Spot。

　　_____

　　＊call 有「打電話」的意思，也有「叫做（什麼）的意思。

9.　Did Grandpa call you this morning?

　　是的，他有打（called）電話給我們。

　　_____

10. Do you like this book?

不，我一點也不喜歡它。

_____ at all.

11. Can you call me tonight?

好，我今晚可以打給你。

_____

12. Can you play the piano?

是的，我會。我每天都彈它。

_____

13. Do you have this book?

是的，我有。我每星期都讀它。

_____

14. Where did you find these two pencils?

我在書桌上找到(found)它們的。

_____

15. How do you like Mr. Lin's English class?

我非常喜歡它。

_____ very much.

16. When do you play the piano?

我每天下午4點彈它。

_____ at 4:00P.M. every day.

17. Who called you this afternoon?

我的父母(parents)今天下午打電話給我。

_____

18. Where did you find this dog?

我在公園裡(in the park)找到牠。

_____

（＊ find 的過去式是 found 。）

19. Did you call your mom this evening?

沒有，我沒有打電話給她。

_____

20. When did you read this English book?

去年我讀了它。

_____

第二課

所有代名詞

在初級本中，我們學會了如何用所有格 my（我的）, your（你的）, his（他的）, her（她的）, its（它、牠的）, your（你們的）, our（我們的）, their（他們的）。

如：my book（我的書）、your sister（你的姊姊）、her brothers（她的兄弟）, our dog（我們的狗）。

如果用所有代名詞來表示這些詞，英文該如何說呢？

2-1 生字

mine	= my+ 名詞	我的
yours	= you+ 名詞	你的
his	= his+ 名詞	他的
hers	= her+ 名詞	她的
ours	= our+ 名詞	我們的
yours	= your+ 名詞	你們的
theirs	= their+ 名詞	他們的
these		這些(this 的複數)
those		那些(that 的複數)
cell phone		手機
flower		花
whose		誰的

Is this your toy car?

這是你的玩具車嗎？

Yes, it's mine.（my toy car）

對，它是我的。

Is that your cell phone?

那是你的手機嗎？

No, it's not mine（my cell phone）; it's hers.（her cell phone）

不，它不是我的；它是她的。

Who gave you these flowers?

誰給你這些花？

These flowers are not mine.（my flowers）They are his.（his flowers）

這些花不是我的。它們是他的。

Whose bikes are those?

那些是誰的腳踏車？

They are ours.（our bikes）

它們是我們的。

Amy's bike is better than our bikes.

愛咪的腳踏車比我們的腳踏車好。

Hers is better than ours.

她的比我們的好。

2-2-1 所有格＋名詞＝所有代名詞

This is my cell phone. → This is mine.

That is her breakfast. → That is hers.

This is your lunch. → This is yours.

This is his dinner. → This is his.

These are our flowers. → These are ours.

Those are your desks. → Those are yours.

These are their bikes. → These are theirs.

This is Amy's coffee. → This is Amy's. → This is hers.

This is my parents' house. → This is my parents'. → This is theirs.

2-3-1 選選看

1.   This is my cell phone. This is _____. （1）mines （2）mine （3）yours

2.   That is your pen. That is _____. （1）yours （2）your （3）hers

3.   Those are my grandma's flowers. Those are _____. （1）his （2）hers （3）mine

4.   This is my brother's bicycle. This is _____. （1）mine （2）ours （3）his

5.   These are my and my sister's books. These are _____. （1）hers （2）mine （3）ours

6.   That is my grandparents' cat. That is _____. （1）theirs （2）it （3）ours

7.   It is your and your mother's computer. It is _____. （1）your （2）yours （3）hers

8.   Those are my cakes. Those are _____. （1）mine （2）theirs （3）ours

9.   This is my parents' house. This is _____. （1）mine （2）ours （3）theirs

10.   These are your dogs. These are _____. （1）your （2）yours （3）its

2-3-2 英文該怎麼說？

1.   Whose cat is this?（這隻貓是誰的？）

      這隻貓是我的。 _____

2. Whose desk is this?

這張桌子是我們的。 _____

3. Whose cell phone is this?

這支手機是她的。 _____

4. Whose flowers are those?

那些花是她們的。 _____

5. Whose car is this?

這輛車是他的。 _____

6. Whose books are these?

這些書是我英文老師的。 _____

7. Whose pencils are those?

那些鉛筆是我父母的。 _____

8. Whose fish is it?

牠是我弟弟的。 _____

9. Whose Coke is it?

它是我朋友的。 _____

10. Whose cakes are these?

這些蛋糕是我們的。 _____

2-3-3 用所有代名詞回答：

例句： Are these your computer games?

　　　 No, they're not mine. They are his.

1. Is this Amy's computer?

No, it isn't _____. It's mine.

2. Are those your grandpa's birds?

Yes, they're _____.

3.   Is that your brother's car?

No, _____. It's my dad's.

4.   Are these the doctor's books ?

No, they _____. They're my teacher's.

5.   Are those my sister's pencils?

Yes, _____.

6.   Are these your friends' bicycles?

No, _____. They are my parents'.

7.   Is this my book?

No, _____. It is Amy's.

8.   Is this your mother's car?

No, _____. It's my father's.

9.   Is this your cell phone?

No, _____. It's my friend's.

10. Are they your（你們的）cats?

No, _____. They are my teacher's.

第三課

我自己、你自己、他自己

—— 反身代名詞

She's talking to herself.

魔鏡、魔鏡……

　　跟朋友談話時我們常會提到我自己如何……，你自己如何……，他自己又如何……。這些「自己」英文該怎麼說呢？

　　有時我們會說「我自己的東西」，「自己的」英文又該如何說呢？

3-1 生字

myself	我自己
yourself	你自己
himself	他自己
herself	她自己
ourselves	我們自己
yourselves	你們自己
themselves	他們自己
my own	我自己的
your own	你自己的
his own	他自己的
use	用（use, used）
with	和（介系詞）
buy	買（buy, bought）
make	做、賺（make, made）
write	寫（write, wrote）

3-2 課文

She's talking to herself.

她正在自言自語。(她在跟自己說話。)

I like to use my own computer; I don't like to use my brother's.

我喜歡用我自己的電腦;我不喜歡用我哥哥的。

He has his own house; he doesn't live with his parents.

他有他自己的房子;他不跟他的父母住。

My daughter bought the piano herself. I didn't buy it for her.

我女兒自己買的鋼琴。我沒有幫她買。

Did you make the bed yourself today?

今天你自己鋪床嗎?

Yes, I made it myself.

對,我自己鋪的。

Did you write this book yourselves?

你們自己寫這本書的嗎？

Yes, we wrote it ourselves.

對，這本書是我們自己寫的。

What is she writing?

她正在寫什麼？

She is writing her own novel.

她正在寫她自己的小說。

Who made this lunch?

誰做的午餐？

He made this lunch himself.

他自己做的午餐。

He makes his own lunch every day.

他每天都自己做午餐。

3-2-1 自己擁有的東西(強調這個東西是自己的)

my own piano 我自己的鋼琴

your own bed 你自己的床

his own desk 他自己的桌子

her own chair 她自己的椅子

its own toy 牠自己的玩具

your own toy car 你們自己的玩具車

our own rooms 我們自己的房間

their own guitars 他們自己的吉他

 3-2-2 強調自己親自做這件事

I make lunch myself. 我自己親自做午餐。

He makes his bed himself every day. 他每天自己鋪床。

She called Amy herself. 她親自打電話給 Amy 。

We will meet her ourselves. 我們會親自見她。

You will come yourselves. 你們會親自來。

They will do it themselves. 他們會自己親自來做。

 3-2-3 -self 的常用語

1.　by -self 獨自

　　I go to school every day by myself. 我每天一個人去上學。(沒有人送也
　　沒有人陪我去)。

Those students made this table by themselves. 那些學生獨力做成這張桌子。

2. for -self 為自己

He made lunch for himself.他為他自己做午餐。

We bought these books for ourselves. 我們為自己買了這些書。

3. Please help yourself. 請自己取用。

Please help yourself to tea. 請自己用茶。

4. Please make yourself at home. 請不要客氣。

＊注意：myself 和 by myself 意思有些不同：

I made this cake myself.（我自己親自做的蛋糕。）

I made this cake by myself.（我自己一個人做成的蛋糕。）

3-3-1 填填看（用 own 來強調是自己的）

1. He does not like _____ _____ computer; he likes his brother's.

2. I have _____ _____ desk.

3. She made _____ _____ bed.

4. Do you have _____ _____ house?

5. The students have _____ _____ pencils.

6. You and your brother have _____ _____ bicycles.

7. We made _____ _____ cake.

8. My grandpa has _____ _____ chair.

9. My friend Amy likes _____ _____ piano.

10. My sons have _____ _____ rooms.

3-3-2 將 myself, yourself, himself, itself, herself, yourselves, themselves, ourselves 填進空格中：

1. My mother made this cake _____.

2. The students did their homework _____.

3. Amy and I wrote this book _____.

4. Did you make lunch for _____?

5. My brother made the bed _____.

6. My grandpa is talking to _____.

7. I like to make breakfast for _____.

8. You and your sister bought the books _____.

9. My aunt went to America by_____.

10. My brother and I played basketball by_____.

3-3-3 英文該如何說？

1. Does your daughter like your house?

   No, she doesn't like mine. 她喜歡她自己的房子。

   _____

2. Did you buy this house?

   No, I didn't. 我的女兒自己買(bought it)。

   _____

3. What does your daughter do every morning?

   她每天早上自己鋪床(make the bed)。

   _____

4. Does she go to school by herself?

   No, she doesn't. 她都跟朋友(with her friends)一起去上學。

   _____

5. Does your daughter have a piano?

   Yes, she does. 她都彈給自己聽(for herself)。

   _____

6. Is that your car?

   No, it isn't. 它是我兒子自己的車。

   _____

7. Does your daughter have a desk?

   Yes, she does. 她有她自己的書桌。

   _____

8. Did you write this book?

   No, I didn't. 我的女兒自己(herself)寫成的。

   _____

9. Did you make this cake?

   No, I didn't. 我的兒子自己一個人做的。

   _____

10. What is your daughter doing?

    她正在自言自語。

    _____

3-3-4 改錯

1. Did you cooked this fish yourself?
2. Did he make this toy car hisself?
3. Is this yourself computer?
4. Do you have yours own bed?
5. Do those your grandma's books?
6. She doesn't have herself computer.
7. They will make a cake by themself.
8. She was made a cake for herself.
9. We made some tea for ourself.
10. I am live here by myself.

第四課

可數和不可數的名詞

There is a bag of rice in the room.

　　中文的名詞語法沒有單數、複數之分，也沒有可數和不可數的不同，我們學英文時常覺得很困擾，不知哪些東西可數（例如：cups, desks, books），哪些不可數（bread, rice, tea, coffee）。

　　其實不可數的東西只要加上可數的單位詞就變得可以數了。例如：water（水）是不可數的名詞，加上 a glass of（一杯，一個玻璃杯）就可以用幾杯來計算了。rice（米）也是不可數的名詞，加上 a bowl of（一碗）或是 a bag of（一袋），也變得可以用幾碗或幾袋來計算了。

4-1 生字

there is	有（單數）
there are	有（複數）
rice	米飯
room	房間
bread	麵包
orange	柳橙
juice	果汁
something	某件東西、某件事情
bowl	碗
a bottle of	一瓶
a piece of	一片，一張（紙）
a glass of	一杯（玻璃杯）
a cup of	一杯（馬克杯、陶瓷杯）
a pot of	一壺
some	一些
please	請

There is a bag of rice in the room.
房間裡有一袋米。

There are two bottles of milk on the table.
桌上有兩瓶牛奶。

I drink some milk and eat some bread for breakfast.
我喝了一些牛奶和吃了一些麵包當早餐。

After dinner, he likes to drink some tea.
吃完晚飯，他喜歡喝些茶。

May I have a glass of orange juice, please?
我可以來一杯柳橙汁嗎？
Here you are. Would you like something to eat?
這是你的果汁。你想吃些什麼嗎？
I'd like a piece of bread.（I'd ＝ I would）
我想吃一片麵包。

My grandpa eats three bowls of rice every day.

我祖父每天吃三碗飯。

My uncle drank two cups of coffee this morning.

我的叔叔今天早上喝了兩杯咖啡。

Who made this pot of black tea?

誰泡的這壺紅茶？（注意：紅茶是 black tea）

I made it myself.

我自己泡的。

May I have a bowl of rice, please?

請給我一碗飯好嗎？

The rice is on the table. Please help yourself.

飯在桌上，請自己盛。

4-2-1 單位詞

一碗	兩碗	一些	許多	一點點
a bowl of rice 一碗飯	two bowls of rice	some rice a little rice	a lot of rice	a little bit of rice
a bag of rice 一袋米	two bags of rice			
a cup of tea 一杯茶	two cups of tea	some tea a little tea	a lot of tea	a little bit of tea
a pot of tea 一壺茶	two pots of tea			
a cup of coffee 一杯咖啡	two cups of coffee	some coffee a little coffee	a lot of coffee	a little bit of coffee
a glass of water 一杯水	two glasses of water	some water a little water	a lot of water	a little bit of water
a glass of milk 一杯牛奶	two glasses of milk	some milk a little milk	a lot of milk	a little bit of milk
a glass of juice 一杯果汁	two glasses of juice	some juice a little juice	a lot of juice	a little bit of juice
a loaf of bread 一條麵包	two loaves of bread	some bread a little bread	a lot of bread	a little bit of bread
a piece of bread 一片(個)麵包	two pieces of bread			
a piece of paper 一張紙	two pieces of paper	some paper	a lot of paper	a little bit of paper

＊a few 和 a little 都是一些(some)的意思，a few 形容可數的東西，例如：
a few books, a few chairs。
a little(一些)形容不可數的東西，例如：a little rice, a little money, a little milk。

＊a loaf(一條) → two loaves(兩條)。當名詞字尾是 f 或 fe 時，複數時 f 或 fe 要改為
ves；如：knife → knives(刀)；life → lives(生命)；leaf → leaves(樹葉)；wife → wives
(妻子)。不過也有例外：roof → roofs(屋頂)。

＊注意：milk, water, juice 通常用玻璃杯裝，單位用 a glass of。coffee, tea 用馬克杯或
瓷杯裝，單位用 a cup of。

4-3 練習題

4-3-1 選選看

1.　I like to drink _____ orange juice every morning. （1）a pot of （2） a bowl of （3）a glass of

2.　My mother made _____ rice for us. （1）some （2）many （3）a

3.　May I have two _____? （1）glass of water （2）glasses of waters （3）glasses of water

4.　The bird eats _____ of rice. （1）a little bit （2）some （3）a lots

5.　There is _____ paper（紙）on the table. （1）a （2）a piece of （3） a lot

6.　The cat drank _____ milk today. （1）a piece of （2）two bowls （3） a lot of

7.　My brother had three _____ this morning. （1）pieces of bread （2）piece of bread （3）pieces of breads

8.　My grandma likes to have _____ tea in the afternoon. （1）a bag of （2）a cup of （3）a bowl of

9.　My father bought two _____ rice. （1）glasses of （2）pots of （3） bags of

10.　A：Who made the cake?　B：I made it _____. （1）myself （2） herself （3）itself

4-3-2 填填看

1. May I have _____ paper? (兩張)
2. My grandma made _____ tea in the afternoon. (一壺)
3. My brother only had _____ rice for lunch. (一碗)
4. I drink _____ milk every day. (一杯)
5. My mother is drinking _____ coffee. (一杯)
6. I only ate _____ bread for breakfast. (一點點)
7. May I have _____ (一杯)milk and _____ (一杯) tea?
8. My sister likes to eat _____ rice in the morning. (一些)
9. There're _____ (三包) rice in the house.
10. My grandpa had an _____ (蛋), _____ (兩片) bread, and _____ (一杯)milk for breakfast.

4-3-3 英文該怎麼說?

1. 有兩張紙在 Amy 的桌上。 There are...

   _____

2. 他晚餐(for dinner)吃了兩碗飯。

   _____

3. 今天早上我的媽媽買了(bought)兩條麵包。

   _____

4. 我可以來杯柳橙汁嗎? May I have..., please?

   _____

5. A:這壺紅茶(black tea)是誰泡的?

B：我自己泡(made)的。

6. 我要一些紙來寫功課(do my homework)。

7. 我每天喝一杯咖啡。

8. 桌上有一杯水。 There is...

9. 我泡了(made)三杯茶。

10. 你想吃點什麼嗎？ Would you like...

4-3-4 改錯

1. I'd like glass of milk.
2. I want to eat two bowl of rice for dinner.
3. She bought some papers last night.
4. He make some tea every morning.
5. My friend made a pot of red tea for me.
6. His parents like to drink some coffees every morning.
7. My grandma does not want to drink a coffee now.
8. There is three bags of rice in the house.
9. Who made two orange juice? My dad did.
10. May I have two bowl of rice, please?

第五課

數詞

在初級本中，我們學了從 0 到 10 的英文說法，現在我們還要繼續學下去，數到 100 為止。大家不要害怕，英文數數有規則可循，例如：

- thirteen（13）, thirty（30）
- fifteen（15）, fifty（50）
- 56 則是 50 加 6 ＝ fifty-six
- 78 則是 70 加 8 ＝ seventy-eight

有趣吧？

5-1 生字

classroom	教室	eighty	80
pocket	口袋	ninety	90
eleven	11	one hundred	100
twelve	12	all together	一共
thirteen	13		
fourteen	14		
fifteen	15		
sixteen	16		
seventeen	17		
eighteen	18		
nineteen	19		
twenty	20		
thirty	30		
forty	40		
fifty	50		
sixty	60		
seventy	70		

5-2 課文

He makes nine hundred NT dollars a day.

他一天賺台幣 900 元

* make 有很多意思：make cakes（做蛋糕），make the bed（鋪床），make money（賺錢），make me happy（使我快樂）

She has thirty-seven students.

她有 37 個學生。

I have twenty NT dollars in my pocket.

我的口袋裡有台幣 20 元。

Last week my uncle gave me fourteen books.

上星期我的伯父給了我 14 本書。

There are fifty-two chairs in the classroom.

教室裡有 52 張椅子。

There are twelve glasses of milk on the table.
桌上有 12 杯牛奶。

There are forty-one students in our class.
我們班上有 41 名學生。

There are sixty-five bowls of rice on the table.
桌上有 65 碗飯。

All together, they drank eighteen cups of tea this morning.
他們今天早上一共喝了 18 杯茶。

All together, he made twenty-one pieces of bread last night.
昨晚他一共做了 21 個麵包。

＊注意：a piece of 可以當「一片」也可以當「一個」來數。

5-3 練習題

5-3-1 數字的英文該怎麼說？

1. I gave her _____ (32) flowers for her birthday.
2. All together, he wrote _____ (11) books.
3. My aunt gave me _____ (87) books.
4. All together, my cousins drank _____ (12) bottles of milk.
5. There are _____ (17) computers in this classroom.
6. She bought _____ (79) books last year.
7. They will meet _____ (46) new students this afternoon.
8. I found _____ (25) cats in the park（公園）.
9. Where can I find my _____ (500) dollars?
10. Who has _____ (92) dollars?

5-3-2　英文該如何說？

1. 這個電腦遊戲是 400 元台幣。

   _____

2. 屋子裡有 80 包米。 There are...

   _____

3. 我的祖母有 11 個茶壺（teapots）。

   _____

4. 今天下午我的學生一共喝了 20 瓶可樂（20 bottles of Coke）。

   _____

5.　我的哥哥給了我 18 本書。

_____

6.　這張書桌是 599 元台幣。

_____

7.　他的英文老師一共有 23 個學生。 All together,...

_____

8.　我媽媽的皮包(bag)裡有 60 元台幣。 There are...

_____

9.　我的姊姊一天賺 900 元台幣。

_____

10.　這位醫生這個月讀了 13 本書。

_____

5-3-3 加加看，一共有多少？減減看，還剩多少？

1.　The cat drank five bowls of milk this morning. The cat drank seven bowls of milk this afternoon.

   All together, the cat drank _____ bowls of milk today.

2.　My grandpa bought twenty flowers. My grandma bought twenty-one flowers.

   All together, my grandparents bought _____ flowers.

3.　My friend drank eight glasses of milk. I drank ten glasses of milk.

   All together, we drank_____ glasses of milk.

4.　She made fifty cups of coffee this morning. He made fifty cups of coffee this morning, too.

   All together, they made_____ cups of coffee.

5.　My father made twelve cakes. My mother made eleven cakes.

All together, they made_____ cakes.

6.　My brother had seventy-three pencils. My brother gave me five pencils.
　　He has_____ pencils now.

7.　There are sixteen boys in the classroom. There are fourteen girls in the classroom.
　　All together, there are _____ students in the classroom.

8.　There are forty-nine pieces of paper on this desk. There are thirty-two pieces of paper on that desk.
　　There are _____ pieces of paper all together.

9.　My sister made ninety NT dollars this morning. She gave me sixty-two NT dollars.
　　She has only_____ NT dollars.

10.　This pen is eighty-four NT dollars. That pen is ten NT dollars.
　　All together, they cost（值）_____ NT dollars.

第六課

數詞的應用

　　上一課我們學會了如何從 1 數到 100，現在來看看如何活用這些數字。

　　在本課中，我們將學習如何問年齡、如何問別人是西元哪一年出生的？不過要記得，年齡通常是西方人的秘密，如果沒有必要，請不要問「你幾歲？」(How old are you?)；不過，問小朋友年齡則沒有關係。

6-1 生字

which	哪一……
year	年
was（were）born	被生出來（因為你已經出生了，所以要用過去式）
husband	丈夫（wife 太太）
old → older than	年紀大 → 年紀比……大
young → younger than	年紀輕 → 年紀比……輕
know	知道（know, knew）
look	看起來（look, looked）

6-2 課文

A : How old are you?

A : 你幾歲？

B : I'm fifty-two years old. How old are you?

B : 我 52 歲。你幾歲？

A : I'm sixty-one years old. You're younger than I.

A : 我 61 歲。你比我年輕。

B : Yes, you are nine years older than I.

B : 是的，你比我大九歲。

A : Which year were you born in?

A : 你是哪一年生的？

B : I was born in 1952. How about you?

B : 我生於 1952 年。你呢？

A : I was born in 1943.

A : 我生於 1943 年。

B : Which year was your husband born in?

B : 你的先生生於哪一年？

A：He was born in 1950.

A：他生於 1950 年。

B：Oh, I didn't know you were older than your husband. You look much younger than he.

B：哦！我不知道你比你的先生還大。你看起來比他年輕多了。

6-2-1 younger than...（比……年輕）
older than...（比……年紀大）

1. She is younger than I.（或than me）
   I am older than she.（或 than her）
2. Amy is older than her husband.
   He is younger than his wife.
3. They are older than we.（或 than us）
   We are younger than they.（或 than them）

6-2-2 大幾歲？

1. She is 5 years older than I.
   I am 5 years younger than she.
2. Amy is 2 years older than her husband.
   He is 2 years younger than his wife.
3. They are 3 years older than we.
   We are 3 years younger than they.

6-3-1 算算看再填

例句：   I am ten years old. You are twelve years old.

    You are two years older than I.

1.   My mom is forty years old. My dad is forty-five years old.

    My mom is _____ than my dad.

2.   My dog is two months old. My cat is six months old.

    My cat is _____ than my dog.

3.   My brother is twenty-two years old. My sister is fifteen years old.

    My sister is _____ than my brother.

4.   Amy is thirty-one years old. Tom is thirty years old.

    Amy is _____ than Tom.

5.   My grandpa is seventy-three years old. My grandma is seventy-seven years old.

    My grandpa is _____ than my grandma.

6.   My teacher is thirty-eight years old. My teacher's husband is forty-one years old.

    My teacher is _____ than her husband.

7.   My cousin is seventeen years old. My cousin's friend is nineteen years old.

    My cousin's friend is _____ than my cousin.

8.   I am twenty-five years old. Henry is twenty-seven years old.

I am _____ than he.

9. My uncle is fifty-three years old. My aunt is fifty-seven years old.

My aunt is _____ than her husband.

10. Your sister is sixteen years old. You are fourteen years old.

You are _____ than she.

6-3-2 填填看

1. How _____ are you? (問年齡)

2. You _____ much younger. (看起來)

3. In which year _____ your sister_____? (哪一年生的？)

4. I _____ born _____ 1978. (1978 年生的)

5. You are three years _____ _____ I. (比我大三歲)

6. I didn't know you _____ older than your brother. (比你弟弟大)

7. He is twenty-seven _____ _____. (27 歲)

8. My husband _____ older than I. (看起來比我大)

9. How _____ you? (你呢？)

10. You _____ beautiful today. (看起來)

6-3-3 改錯

1. How old are your brother?

2. He is three years old than I.

3. You sister is younger than me.

4. Their brother born in Taipei.

5. I went to America at 1997.

6. You are look very happy.

7.   You mom is older than my mom.

8.   In which year were your husband born?

9.   I didn't know you were younger than you wife.

10.   She is look younger than her sister.

6-3-4 中文該如何說?

1.   你的祖母幾歲?

    _____

2.   她的狗看起來很悲傷(sad)。

    _____

3.   我的貓看起來比你的貓老。

    _____

4.   這本書比那本書舊(older)。

    _____

5.   他的太太看起來很年輕。

    _____

6.   我的祖父生於 1926 年。

    _____

7.   他的父親今年93歲。(阿拉伯數字請用英文寫出來。)

    _____

8.   你的先生是哪一年生的?(Which year...)

    _____

9.   哪一隻狗年紀比較大?

    _____

10.   他看起來比80歲年輕。(...than eighty years old)

    _____

第七課

多少？

（How much...? How many...?）

How much chicken would you like?

　　我們常聽人問：「多少錢？」、「多少個蘋果？」，雖然都是「多少」，但因為涉及可數和不可數（錢 [money] 是不可數的名詞；蘋果 [apple] 是可數的名詞），於是「多少」就有 How much...?（不可數）與 How many...?（可數）的不同。

　　How much ＋不可數名詞

　　How many ＋可數名詞

　　下面的名詞哪些可數？哪些不可數？請猜猜看。

7-1 生字

pizza	披薩
chicken	雞肉
pork	豬肉
apple	蘋果
banana	香蕉
mango	芒果
melon	香瓜
watermelon	西瓜
just	剛才
ice cream	冰淇淋
scoop	(幾)球(數冰淇淋的單位)
box (boxes)	盒子

How much pizza did you eat for lunch?

你吃了多少披薩當午餐？

I only ate three pieces of pizza.

我只吃了 3 片披薩。

Do you like chicken or pork?

你喜歡雞肉還是豬肉？

I like chicken better.

我比較喜歡雞肉。

How much chicken would you like?

你要多少雞肉？

I'd like two pieces.

我想要兩塊。

* would you like 是問別人想要什麼東西時客氣的問法。回答時也可以用 I would
　like...或簡寫成 I'd like...。

How much fruit would you like?

你要多少水果？

I'd like two apples, five mangos, four melons, and some bananas.

我要兩個蘋果、5個芒果、4個香瓜和一些香蕉。

How many pieces of watermelon did you just eat?

你剛才吃了幾片西瓜？

I only ate two pieces.

我只吃了兩片。

How much ice cream did you just eat?

你剛才吃了多少冰淇淋？

I only ate two scoops of ice cream.

我只吃了兩球冰淇淋。

She ate two boxes of ice cream.

她吃了兩盒冰淇淋。

How many pieces of paper do you have?

你有幾張紙？

I have twenty-eight pieces.

我有28張。

＊注意：紙張也可用 "sheet" 計算，例如：I have two sheets of paper.

 7-2-1 圖表

How much money do you have?	I only have forty-three dollars.
How much ice cream did he eat?	He ate two scoops of ice cream.
How much rice would you like?	I'd like two bowls.
How much milk would you like?	I'd like two glasses.
How much chicken did you eat for lunch?	I ate a lot (很多).
How much pork did she eat today?	She only ate one piece.

How many mangos did you eat?	I ate two mangos.
How many watermelons do you have in your bag?	I have two watermelons.
How many beds are there in your room?	There are two beds in my room.
How many desks are there in the classroom?	There are fifteen desks.
How many bags do you have?	I have two bags.
How many basketballs do you have?	I only have one.

7-3 練習題

7-3-1 填填看：用 How much 還是用 How many?

1. _____ pieces of cake did you eat yesterday?

2. _____ money did you make last week?

3. _____ ice cream did my sister eat?

4. _____ pieces of paper do you have?

5. _____ fruit did my mom buy?

6. _____ bags of rice are there in the room?

7. _____ chicken would you like?

8. _____ pizza did my brother and his friends eat today?

9. _____ boxes of apples did my grandma give us?

10. _____ mangos are there on the table?

11. _____ fish did you eat?

12. _____ books did you buy?

13. _____ chairs do you have?

14. _____ water do you drink every day?

15. _____ cups of coffee did you drink yesterday?

7-3-2 看圖畫回答問題（請詳答）

1. How many watermelons are there in the box?

2. How much money do you have in your pocket?

 3. How many beds are there in your sister's room?

 4. How many bowls of rice did you have for dinner?

 5. How much fruit did your mom buy?

 6. How much pizza did the students have for lunch?

 7. How many brothers and sisters do you have?

 8. How much pork did your father eat for dinner?

 9. How much ice cream did she just eat?

 10. How many bowls of milk did the cat have?

7-3-3 英文該如何回答？

1.   How many glasses of water do you drink every day?

我每天喝 8 杯水。

_____

2.   What would your grandpa like to eat for lunch?

他想吃一些(some)豬肉。

_____

3. How many books do you have?

我一共有 35 本書。

_____

4. How many bowls of rice did your sister eat for dinner?

她只吃了一碗飯。

_____

5. How much ice cream did you just eat?

我剛剛只吃了 3 球冰淇淋。

_____

6. How many pieces of watermelon did they eat after lunch?

他們一共吃了 11 片西瓜。

_____

7. How much fruit would you like?

我想要兩個芒果(mangos)和 3 條香蕉(bananas)。

_____

8. How many pieces of pizza would you like?

我想要 4 片披薩。

_____

9. How many scoops of ice cream did your dad eat this afternoon?

他只吃了一球冰淇淋。

_____

10. How much chicken would you like?

我想要兩塊(two pieces of)雞排。

_____

第八課

詞類變化：
名詞、動詞、形容詞、副詞

My aunt is very angry now.

英文和中文一樣，有許多不同的詞類。例如我說：「我很健康」，這裡的「健康」是形容詞；如果我說：「我關心你的健康」，這裡的「健康」就成了名詞。雖然中文都是說「健康」，英文說法卻不盡相同。

我們在「初級本」中學了一些名詞、動詞和形容詞，本課我們再學一個詞類：副詞，副詞是用來形容動詞和形容詞。我們現在來看看這些詞類該如何靈活運用。

8-1 生字

anger	生氣（名詞）
angry	生氣的（形容詞）
angrily	生氣地（副詞）
happiness	快樂（名詞）
happy	快樂的（形容詞）
happily	快樂地（副詞）
health	健康（名詞）
healthy	健康的（形容詞）
healthily	健康地（副詞）
talk to	跟……說話（talk, talked）
child	小孩（children 是小孩的複數）
stop	停止（stop, stopped）
care about	關心（care, cared）
should	應該

My aunt is very angry now.

我的阿姨現在很生氣。

She is talking to her children angrily.

她正生氣地跟孩子說話。

She can't stop her anger.

她不能停止她的生氣。

My grandma is happy every day.

我的祖母每天都很快樂。

Her dog is happy, too.

她的狗也很快樂。

They live happily together.

他們快樂地住在一起。

Their happiness makes us happy, too.

他們的快樂讓我們也快樂。

My grandpa is very healthy, but his friends all have bad health.

我的祖父很健康,但是他朋友的健康狀況都不好。

He eats healthily.

他吃得很健康。

We should care about our own health.

我們應該關心我們自己的健康。

 8-2-1 圖表

名詞	形容詞	副詞
happiness 快樂	happy	happily
anger 生氣	angry	angrily
health 健康	healthy	healthily
humor 幽默	humorous	humorously
laziness 懶惰	lazy	lazily
craziness 瘋狂	crazy	crazily
slowness 慢	slow	slowly
success 成功	successful	successfully
hardness 硬度	hard 硬；難	*hard 努力

＊注意：hardly 是「幾乎不」的意思，例如：I hardly ever smoke.（我幾乎不抽煙。）；
　　與 "work hard" 的 hard 意思無關聯。

 8-2-2 make 的用法：某件事或某個人讓人……

· He makes us happy. 他讓我快樂。
· She makes him angry. 她讓他生氣。
· This book makes them successful. 這本書使他們成功。
· This song makes me crazy. 這首歌使我瘋狂。(I am crazy about this song.
　的意思則是指「我非常喜歡這首歌」。)
· They make it slow. 他們使它變慢。
· This book makes her healthy. 這本書使她健康。

8-2-3 care about 關心

What do you care about? 你關心什麼？（care 是動詞，問句要用 do）
- I care about my parents' health. 我關心我父母的健康。
- I care about my family. 我關心我的家人。
- I care about my grandpa and grandma. 我關心我的祖父母。
- I care about my friends. 我關心我的朋友。
- I care about my dog. 我關心我的狗。

 8-2-4 be crazy about 指非常喜某人或某件事情

What are you crazy about?（crazy 是形容詞，問句要用 be 動詞）
- I'm crazy about that singer. 我太喜歡那個歌星。
- I'm crazy about that song. 我太喜歡那首歌。
- I'm crazy about that book. 我太喜歡那本書。
- I'm crazy about that movie. 我太喜歡那部電影。

8-3 練習題

8-3-1 選選看

1.　The bird is singing _____. (1) happy　(2) happily　(3) angry

2.　My parents have good _____. (1) health　(2) healthily　(3) healthy

3.　My sister cannot stop her _____. (1) angry　(2) anger　(3) angrily

4.　The teacher is talking _____ to his students. (1) angry　(2) anger　(3) angrily

5.　She eats her dinner _____. (1) slower　(2) slowly　(3) slow

6.　I care about my grandfather's_____. (1) happy　(2) happily　(3) happiness

7.　Amy wants to be _____. (1) health　(2) healthily　(3) healthy

8.　My brother and I walk to school _____ every morning. (1) slowly　(2) slow　(3) slowness

9.　David is a _____ boy. (1) happily　(2) happy　(3) happiness

10.　Amy wants to be _____. (1) success　(2) successful　(3) successfully

11.　He doesn't care about his _____. (1) healthy　(2) health　(3) healthily

12.　They dance（跳舞）_____. (1) crazily　(2) craze　(3) crazy

13.　My English teacher is very _____. (1) humor　(2) humorous　(3) humorously

14.　You should go to school _____. (1) happiness　(2) anger　(3)

happily

15. My students are not _____. (1) lazy (2) laziness (3) lazily

16. His son's _____ makes them happy. (1) success (2) successful (3) successfully

17. His _____ makes us angry. (1) slowly (2) slowness (3) slow

18. He is a happy boy, but he is a little bit _____. (1) lazy (2) laziness (3) lazily

19. Their daughter's laziness makes them _____. (1) angrily (2) angry (3) anger

20. Their children don't care about their _____. (1) happy (2) happily (3)happiness

8-3-2 填填看

1. My sister does her homework_____ (slow) every night.

2. My cousin is singing a song _____. (happy)

3. His grandson is a _____ (happy) boy.

4. My children are very _____. (healthy)

5. My grandma eats _____. (healthy)

6. We care about my grandpa's _____. (healthy)

7. My mother is _____ now. (angry)

8. My mother is talking _____ to my father. (angry)

9. My father cannot stop his _____. (angry)

10. My students are singing _____. (crazy)

11. Amy is a _____ singer. (crazy)

12. Her _____ makes us happy. (crazy)

13. Amy is a _____ mother. (successful)

14. Her _____ makes us happy. (successful)

15. She does her work _____. (successful)

16. I made this cake _____.(successful)

17. Her students are very _____. (lazy)

18. Their _____ makes her angry. (lazy)

19. My grandpa takes a shower _____. (slow)

20. He writes very _____.(slow)

8-3-3 改錯

1. I care about my sister's healthy.

2. My parents eat health.

3. My father is successfully.

4. Amy and her brother are talking happy.

5. I can't stop my angrily.

6. We care about our own healthy.

7. My brother is calling (打電話) his friend angry.

8. The children are singing happy.

9. He is crazy reading books.

10. I walk to school slow.

11. Amy learns English (學英文) crazy.

12. I don't like his anger dog.

13. They are happiness boys and girls.

14. Who is care about my happiness?

15. Why are your students so craze?

16. Why don't you care about your healthy?

17. Who is that slowly boy?

18. How do you like that happiness girl?
19. I crazy about that movie.
20. Why did you talk angry?
21. I am care about my friends.
22. Are you care about Amy?
23. I am craze about this computer game.
24. He is make his bed slowly.
25. She is play the piano crazily.

第九課

動名詞和不定詞

（動詞＋ing 和 to ＋動詞）

I finished reading this book
last night.

我們在初級本中談到，如果有兩個動詞，之間一定要加 to。
例如：

· I like to read books.（我喜歡看書。）

· He wants to play computer games.（他要玩電腦遊戲）。

to read, to play 前面加 to 的動詞，都叫做不定詞。

至於動名詞則是動詞後面接 ing 的詞，例如：reading, playing。

有的動詞後面一定要接不定詞，有的動詞後面一定要接動名詞，有的則是可以接不定詞，也可以接動名詞。

例如：

· I want to do my homework now.

我現在要寫功課了。（動詞 want 的後面只能接不定詞──to do）

· I finished reading this book last night.

我昨晚讀完這本書了。（動詞 finish 的後面只能接動名詞──reading）

· I like to read books.

我喜歡讀書。

I like fo read books. 也可以寫成 I like reading books. 兩句意思一樣。to read 是不定詞，reading 是動名詞。like 後面可以接不定詞(to + 動詞)，也可以接動名詞(動詞 + ing)。

9-1 生字

cousin	堂、表兄弟姊妹
grandchild	孫子女，外孫子女（複數為 grandchildren）
granddaughter	孫女，外孫女
grandson	孫子、外孫
novel	小說
enjoy	享受，喜歡（enjoy, enjoyed）
finish	完成（finish, finished）
want	要（want, wanted）
decide	決定（decide, decided）
stop	停止（stop, stopped）

＊ stop 字尾是「子音＋母音＋子音」(t＋o＋p)，過去式加 ed 時要重複子音 p
　　→ stopped。

His cousins like to play cards.

他的表兄弟姊妹喜歡玩撲克牌。

They like playing cards.

他們喜歡玩撲克牌。

My teacher's granddaughter likes to read books.

我老師的孫女喜歡看書。

She likes reading novels.

她喜歡看小說。

She doesn't enjoy cooking. She enjoys reading books.

她不喜歡烹飪，她喜歡看書。

His grandson finished doing his homework at 8:00 P.M. tonight.

他的孫子今晚8點寫完了功課。

I want to see that movie, but I don't want to go with him.

我要去看那部電影，但是我不想跟他去。

I decided to go by myself.

我決定自己一個人去。

He stopped to drink coffee.

他停下來喝咖啡。

He stopped drinking coffee.

他不再喝咖啡了。（他戒喝咖啡了。）

＊注意：stop 後面雖可以接不定詞，也可以接動名詞，不過意思卻不相同。

9-2-1 動詞後面可以加動名詞也可以加不定詞：

begin to read 開始看書
begin reading 開始看書

like to walk 喜歡走路
like walking 喜歡走路

hate to study 討厭讀書
hate studying 討厭讀書

love to play the piano 愛彈鋼琴
love playing the piano 愛彈鋼琴

 9-2-2 動詞後面只能加不定詞：

want to go home 要回家
decide to walk home 決定走路回家
agree to see a movie 同意去看一部電影
plan to drive home 計畫開車回家

 9-2-3 動詞後面只能加動名詞：

enjoy sleeping 喜歡（享受）睡覺
keep listening to music 一直聽音樂

＊ keep 有保持某個動作的意思，例如：He keeps looking at me. 他一直在看著我。

finish making the bed 鋪完床

9-3-1 填填看：請填上不定詞或動名詞？

1. My mother enjoys_____.(cook)

2. The students began_____ (read) in the classroom.

3. I finished_____ (do) my homework in the afternoon.

4. Amy and David like_____ (play) cards.

5. My father wants_____ (see) that picture.

6. My parents decided_____ (see) a movie this afternoon.

7. My brother likes_____ (read) novels.

8. My sister loves_____ (play) the piano.

9. The dog keeps_____ (look) at me.

10. My cousin hates_____ (study) English.

11. Amy enjoys _____ (learn) English.

12. My grandma decided _____ (learn) to use the computer.
    （學習用電腦）

13. My dad agrees _____ (drive) me to school.

14. My grandpa stopped _____ (drink) coffee last year. He
    doesn't like to drink coffee.

15. I stopped _____ (eat) ice cream.（戒吃冰淇淋）

9-3-2 改錯：

1. My brother didn't finish make the bed.

2.　The dog wants go home.

3.　I like to walking to school.

4.　My father doesn't enjoy to cook.

5.　My cousins like play cards.

6.　My grandmother decided making cookies this afternoon.

7.　My sister keeps listen to music at night.

8.　My grandfather agreed seeing a movie with me.

9.　I decided go by myself.

10.　The birds began to singing in the morning.

11.　He is keep talking to me.

12.　I am not enjoy studying English.

13.　He likes eat a lot of fruit.

14.　They do not like drink orange juice.

15.　She wanted eating some rice and chicken.

9-3-3 英文該怎麼說？

1.　What does your brother hate to do?

　　我的哥哥討厭學數學（study math）。

　　_____

2.　What did your mom begin to do?

　　我的媽媽開始讀一本小說。

　　_____

3.　What does Amy's cat like?

　　Amy 的貓喜歡喝牛奶。

　　_____

4.　What do your friends like to do?

我的朋友喜歡喝下午茶(afternoon tea)。

_____

5.　What did your daughter begin to do today?

我的女兒今天開始彈鋼琴。

_____

6.　What do your cousins enjoy doing?

我的表兄弟喜歡玩撲克牌。

_____

7.　What does your dad hate doing?

我的爸爸討厭開車去上班(to work)。

_____

8.　What does your uncle like to eat?

他喜歡吃米飯(rice)。

_____

9.　What does David's dog enjoy doing?

David 的狗喜歡睡午覺(take a nap)。

_____

10.　What does your grandma like to make?

她喜歡做餅乾(cookies)。

_____

第十課

總是、經常和不常

I seldom eat breakfast.

　　我們跟朋友聊天時，常常會問：「你多久去一次圖書館？」(How often do you go to the library?)、「你多久看一次電影？」(How often do you go to see a movie?)、「我經常……」(I often...)、「我很少……」(I seldom...)、「我總是……」(I always...)、「我從不……」(I never...)、「我有時……」(I sometimes...)。

　　用這些字句時，通常都是表達個人的習慣，可以用現在式、過去式或未來式來表示。

　　例如：

· We often played chess when we were children.

　　我們小的時候常常下棋。（過去的習慣）

· I usually go to the library after lunch.

　　我通常午餐後去圖書館。（現在的習慣）

· I will always miss you.

　　我會永遠想念你。（道別時說的話，指未來的情況）

　　我們這一課談的都是個人目前的生活作息，一概用現在式來表示。

10-1 生字

always	總是
usually	通常
often	經常
sometimes	有時
seldom	很少
hardly ever	幾乎不
never	絕不，從來不
strange	奇怪
any	任何
wife	太太
husband	先生
go to bed	上床睡覺
get up	起床
sleep late	睡到很晚才起床

＊ sleep late 這句話常遭人誤解為睡得晚，睡得晚的英文是：go to bed very late。

I seldom eat breakfast.
我很少吃早餐。

She sometimes likes to eat an apple in the afternoon.
她有時喜歡在下午吃一個蘋果。

My cousins usually go to see a movie on weekends.
我的表兄弟姊妹通常在週末（星期六或日）看電影。

They always enjoy listening to music at night.
他們總是喜歡晚上聽音樂。

It's strange. He never eats any chicken.
好奇怪。他從不吃（任何）雞肉。

She hardly ever drinks milk.
她幾乎不喝牛奶。

His wife often goes to bed at 11:00 P.M.
他的太太常常晚上 11 點上床。

She never gets up before 8:00 A.M.
她從來沒有早上 8 點以前起床。

She always sleeps late.
她總是睡到很晚才起床。

Her husband always makes the bed.
總是她先生鋪床。

They usually go to the library after dinner.
他們通常吃完晚飯去圖書館。

10-2-1 程度的差異

never (0%)

I never enjoy reading comic books.

我從不喜歡看漫畫書。

hardly ever (10%)

I hardly ever get up after 8:00 A.M.

我幾乎沒有 8 點以後才起床。

seldom (20%)

I seldom study English at night.

我很少晚上念英文。

sometimes (50%)

I sometimes sleep late on Sundays.

我有時星期天會很晚才起床。

often (70%)

I often like to walk to school.

我常常喜歡走路去上學。

usually (80%)

I usually go to the bookstore after school.

我放學後通常會去書店。

always (100%)

I always go to Taichung by bus.

我總是搭巴士去台中。

10-3 練習題

10-3-1 請說出你個人和父母的生活習慣，什麼是你們經常做的事？什麼是你們幾乎不做的事？什麼是你們有時會做的事？什麼又是你們從不做的事？

1. I never _____.
2. I hardly ever_____.
3. I seldom _____.
4. I sometimes _____.
5. I often _____.
6. I usually _____.
7. I always _____.
8. My dad never _____.
9. My mom hardly ever_____.
10. My dad sometimes _____.
11. My mom never _____.
12. My parents often _____.

10-3-2 填填看：

1. My grandma _____ drinks any coffee.（幾乎不）
2. My sister _____ gets up before eight. （從未）
3. I _____ play the piano. （很少）

4. My parents _____ like to go to see movies by themselves. (有時)

5. My brother _____ plays computer games at night. (通常)

6. My cat _____ drinks milk in the morning. (總是)

7. I usually_____ at 10:00P.M. (上床)

8. My grandfather always_____ before 7:00 A.M. (起床)

9. David _____ eats beef(牛肉). (從不)

10. My mother doesn't like to _____. (晚起床)

11. My teacher _____ eats an apple in the afternoon. (經常)

12. I _____ walk to school. (通常是)

13. It's _____. (奇怪) She doesn't have any friends.

14. I _____ read any novels.(幾乎不)

15. My uncle _____ eats a lot of pork(吃很多豬肉). (常常)

10-3-3 英文該怎麼說？

1. 他從不吃早餐。

    _____

2. 我的媽媽常常打電話給我的外祖母(英文祖母和外祖母都是 grandma)。

    _____

3. 他的祖父從不晚起(sleep late)。

    _____

4. Amy 的鳥很少喝水。

    _____

5. 我的阿姨常常去日本(Japan)。

    _____

6. 她的舅舅總是搭巴士去台南(Tainan)。

7. 你總是 7 點以前起床嗎？

8. 我的父母幾乎不吃豬肉。

9. 你很少喝可樂嗎？

10. 他們通常會在晚餐後吃冰淇淋(ice cream)。

第十一課

現在完成式

（介紹動詞三態變化）

I have met her in the park.

　　我們中國人打招呼時，常問對方「吃飽沒有？」；聊天時，有時也會問別人「讀過這本書沒有？」、「去過大陸沒有？」；這些問對方「已經」做完了什麼事，或問對方有沒有類似的「經驗」，都要用「現在完成式」來表示。

　　本課我們會介紹動詞三態的變化：

　1. 第一種時態是動詞原形，如：

　　I meet her at school every day.（我每天都會在學校見到她。）

　　I will meet her tomorrow.（我明天會跟她見面。）

　2. 第二種時態是過去式，如：

　　I met her last night.（我昨晚見過她了。）

　3. 第三種時態是過去分詞，如：

　　Have you met?（你們已經見過面了嗎？）

＊現在完成式是 have 或 has ＋ 動詞第三時態（過去分詞）

＊現在完成式的問句：Have you met?

＊現在完成式的否定句：We have not met yet. 或是 We haven't met yet.

11-1 生字

year	年
ago	之前（例：three years ago 三年前）
park	公園
yet	迄今

以下是動詞三態變化：

1. meet,	2. met,	3. met	遇到
1. read,	2. read,	3. read	閱讀（read 雖然三態同型，但讀音不同）
1. eat,	2. ate,	3. eaten	吃
1. go,	2. went,	3. gone	去
1. see,	2. saw,	3. seen	看
1. live,	2. lived,	3. lived	住
1. learn,	2. learned,	3. learned	學習

Has he read this English book yet?

他讀過這本書嗎？（現在完成式）

Yes, he has.

是的，他讀過。（現在完成式）

When did he read it?

他什麼時候讀的？（過去式）

He read it three years ago.

他三年前讀的。（過去式）

Have you met yet?

你們見過面了嗎？（現在完成式）

Yes, we have.

是的，我們見過。（現在完成式）

Where did you meet?

你們在那裡見面的？（過去式）

We met in the park last night.

我們昨晚在公園見面的。（過去式）

Have you seen this movie yet?

你看過這部電影了嗎？（現在完成式）

No, I haven't seen that movie yet.

沒有，我還沒有看那部電影。（現在完成式）

I will see it next week.

我下星期會看。（未來式）

Have you been to China yet?

你去過中國嗎？（現在完成式）

Yes, I have.

是的，我去過。（現在完成式）

When did you go there?

你什麼時候去的？（過去式）

I went there two months ago.

我兩個月前去的。（過去式）

11-3 動詞三態變化表：

動詞三態變化有規則變化和不規則變化兩種，規則的很簡單，只要加 ed 就好了，不規則的除了靠背誦，沒有其他方法。

 ## 11-3-1 規則變化表：

動詞原形	動詞過去式	動詞過去分詞
finish	finished	finished
cook	cooked	cooked
help	helped	helped
listen	listened	listened
play	played	played
walk	walked	walked
learn	learned	learned
wash	washed	washed
decide	decided	decided
hate	hated	hated
like	liked	liked
love	loved	loved
live	lived	lived
stop	stopped	stopped
study	studied	studied

＊ stop 的 o 是母音、p 是子音，字尾是母音＋子音，加 ed 時要重複 p → stopped。

＊ study 的 y 的前面是子音 d，加 ed 時要把 y 變成 i → studied。

＊ play 的 y 的前面是母音 a，加 ed 時 y 保持不變 → played。

11-3-2 不規則變化表：

動詞原形	動詞過去式	動詞過去分詞
do	did	done
is, are	was, were	been
have, has	had	had
make	made	made
eat	ate	eaten
find	found	found
see	saw	seen
drink	drank	drunk
buy	bought	bought
take	took	taken
come	came	come
give	gave	given
write	wrote	written
keep	kept	kept
meet	met	met
sleep	slept	slept
sing	sang	sung

11-4-1 現在完成式問句圖表：

Have	I	met him yet?
Have	you	taken a shower yet?
Has	she	called her mom yet?
Has	he	walked the dog yet?
Has	it	drunk any milk yet?
Have	we	been here yet?
Have	you	washed your hands yet?
Have	they	done the dishes yet?

 11-4-2 現在完成式否定句圖表：

I	haven't met him yet.
You	haven't taken a shower yet.
She	hasn't called her mom yet.
He	hasn't walked the dog yet.
It	hasn't drunk its milk yet.
We	haven't been there yet.
You	haven't washed your hands yet.
They	haven't done the dishes yet.

11-5-1 填填看：

1. A：Have we met?

   B：Yes, _____.

   A：When did we meet?

   B：_____（one year ago）

   A：Where _____ we meet?

   B：_____（at school）

2. A：_____ you read this novel yet?

   B：No, I haven't. _____（read it tomorrow）

3. A：_____ David been to America?

   B：Yes, he _____.

   A：When _____ he go there?

   B：He _____ there three weeks ago.

4. A：_____ your cousins played the piano yet?

   B：Yes, they have.

   A：When _____ they play the piano?

   B：They _____ it at 3:00 P.M.

5. A：_____ your grandchildren learned English?

   B：Yes, they have.

A：When did they learn it?

B：They _____ it two years ago.

11-5-2 選選看

1. I haven't _____ that movie yet. （1）see （2）saw （3）seen
2. _____ Amy learned English? （1）Had （2）Has （3）Have
3. She _____ see the movie next week. （1）is （2）has （3）will
4. _____ your brother read this book? （1）Have （2）Is （3）Has
5. We _____ in the park last night. （1）met （2）meet （3）have met
6. Amy _____ Chinese three years ago. （1）have learned （2）learned （3）has learn
7. Have your grandparents _____ to China? （1）be （2）been （3）go
8. My mother _____ lunch. （1）has cooking （2）has cook （3）has cooked
9. My cats _____ a nap. （1）have took （2）have taken （3）have take
10. I played the piano three years _____. （1）ago （2）now （3）after

11-5-3　英文該如何說？

1. 她兩年前遇見過（met）這位歌星。

   _____

2. 我還沒有學英文（yet）。

   _____

3. 我的哥哥已經睡過午覺了。

   _____

4. 我的姊姊已經去過美國了。

5.　我的姊姊還沒有讀過這本小說。

6.　明天我會騎腳踏車(ride the bicycle)去上學。

7.　我的祖父母從來沒有去過中國。

8.　他今天沒有彈鋼琴。

9.　我的貓還沒有喝牛奶。

10.　你的爸爸已經洗了碗(do the dishes)。

11-5-4 改錯

1. Has your parents been to America?
2. He hasn't do the dishes yet.
3. My grandpa have been to Japan.
4. He goes there eleven years ago.
5. Have you eat fruit yet?
6. When did you played the piano?
7. Have you buy a new car yet?
8. Mr. Lin hasn't wrote letters to his students.
9. I hasn't finished my homework yet.
10. I have find a good novel.

第十二課

How long...?

現在完成進行式

How long have you been learning English?

我們常問人：「你們學英文學多久了？」、「你在台中住了多久？」這個「多久」(How long)是表示從過去繼續到現在且一直持續的動作或狀態，沒有間斷，可以用「現在完成進行式」來表示:

have + been + 動詞 ing

has + been + 動詞 ing

例如：

· How long have you been learning English?

你學英文學多久了？

· I have been learning English for six years.

我學英文有 6 年。（現在還在學。）

· I have been learning English since I was twelve years old.

我從 12 歲開始學英文的。

"How long" 通常都用「現在完成進行式」來表達，但有些動詞如：believe, be, cost, hate, have, know, like, love, own, buy, see...，沒有持續進行的意思，所以只能用「現在完成式」來表達，不能用「現在完成進行式」。

· I have known her for 30 years. 我認識她已 30 年了。

· I have been here for an hour. 我到這裡已經 1 小時了。

· I haven't seen you for a long time. 我好久沒有見到你了。

12-1 生字

since	自從
wait for	等待（wait, waited, waited, waiting）
how long	多久
rain	下雨（rain, rained, rained, raining）
the day before yesterday	前天
teach	教（teach, taught, taught, teaching）
talk	說話（talk, talked, talked, talking）
hour	小時
o'clock	（幾）點鐘
live	住（live, lived, lived, living）
kid	小孩

12-2 課文

How long have you been waiting for the bus?

你等巴士等多久了？

I have been waiting for the bus for an hour.

我已經等巴士等了一小時了。（車還沒來。）

I've been waiting for the bus since 3 o'clock this afternoon.

我從今天下午３點開始等巴士。

How long has it been raining?

雨已經下多久了？

It has been raining for three days.

雨已經下了３天了。（現在還沒停。）

It has been raining since the day before yesterday.

前天開始下雨。

How long has she been taking a shower?

她洗澡已經洗多久了？

She has been taking a shower for 30 minutes.

她已經洗了 30 分鐘了。（現在還在洗。）
She has been taking a shower since 9:30 P.M.
她從晚上 9:30 開始洗的。

How long have you been teaching English?
你英文教了多久了？
I have been teaching English for twenty-five years.
我教英文已教了 25 年了。（現在還在教。）
I have been teaching English since 1979.
我從 1979 年開始教英文。

How long have they been living here?
他們在這裡住多久了？
They have been living here for fifteen years.
他們在這裡已住了 15 年。（他們現在還住在這裡。）
They have been living here since they were little kids.
從他們還是小孩的時候就住在這裡了。

12-3 動詞 + ing 的規則

1. 動詞最後一個字母是 e：take → taking（去 e 加 ing）
2. 動詞後兩字母是一母音、一子音：stop → stopping（重複子音加 ing）
3. 動詞後兩字母是一母音、一子音(子音是 y)：play → playing（不需重複子音 y）
4. 動詞後三字母是兩母音、一子音：rain→raining（不需重複子音，只加 ing）

 ## 12-4 since 和 for 的用法：

1.　How long have you been learning Japanese? 你學日文學多久了？
　　I've been learning it for five years. (＊ I've = I have)
　　I've been learning it since five years ago. 從 5 年前開始學。

2.　How long has he been talking to Ms. Lin? 他跟林女士談話談多久了？
　　He's been talking to her for one hour. (＊ He's = He has)
　　He's been talking to her since one hour ago.從 1 小時前開始談。

3.　How long has it been drinking milk? 牠喝牛奶喝多久了？
　　It's been drinking milk for fifteen minutes. (分鐘) (＊ It's = It has)
　　It's been drinking milk since fifteen minutes ago. 從 15 分鐘前開始喝。

4.　How long have you and your sister been studying English?
　　你和你姊姊念英文念多久了？
　　We've been studying English for two hours. (＊ We've = We have)
　　We've been studying English since two hours ago.從兩小時前開始念。

5.　How long have you (你們) been listening to the radio?
　　你們聽收音機聽多久了？
　　We've been listening to the radio for an hour. (＊ We've = We have)

We've been listening to the radio since an hour ago.

從 1 小時前開始聽。

6.　How long have they been working? 他們工作多久了？

They've been working for six years. (＊ They've = They have)

They've been working since six years ago. 6 年前開始工作。

 12-5 縮寫

I have been riding...	→	I've been riding...
You have been writing...	→	You've been writing...
He has been singing...	→	He's been singing...
She has been reading...	→	She's been reading...
It has been sleeping...	→	It's been sleeping...
We have been eating...	→	We've been eating...
You have been learning...	→	You've been learning...
They have been drinking...	→	They've been drinking...

12-6-1 填填看

1.　How long have you been ＿＿＿＿＿＿＿＿ （eat）?
2.　How long have you been ＿＿＿＿＿＿＿＿ （drive）?
3.　How long has she been＿＿＿＿＿＿＿＿ （play）the piano?
4.　How long has it been＿＿＿＿＿＿＿＿ （sleep）?
5.　How long have they been＿＿＿＿＿＿＿＿ （read）books?
6.　How long have they been＿＿＿＿＿＿＿＿ （study）?
7.　How long has he been＿＿＿＿＿＿＿＿ （take）a shower?
8.　How long have you been＿＿＿＿＿＿＿＿ （listen）to music?
9.　How long has your mom been＿＿＿＿＿＿＿＿ （take）a nap?
10.　How long has he been＿＿＿＿＿＿＿＿ （talk）on the cell phone?
11.　How long have they been＿＿＿＿＿＿＿＿ （write）e-mails?（電子郵件）
12.　How long has your uncle been ＿＿＿＿＿＿＿＿ （talk）to his friends?
13.　How long has your teacher been＿＿＿＿＿＿＿＿ （teach）English?
14.　How long have you been＿＿＿＿＿＿＿＿ （do）your homework?
15.　How long have they been＿＿＿＿＿＿＿＿ （drink）coffee?

12-6-2 用 since 還是用 for?

1. I've been learning English ＿＿＿＿＿＿＿＿ three years.
2. She's been talking on the phone ＿＿＿＿＿＿＿＿ an hour.
3. He's been eating lunch ＿＿＿＿＿＿＿＿ one o'clock this afternoon.

4. I've been doing my homework _____ thirty minutes.

5. We've been living here _____ I was very young.（我很小的時候）

6. They've been playing baseball _____ three o'clock.

7. I've been talking to my teacher _____ twenty minutes ago.

8. We've been playing computer games _____ forty minutes.

9. She's been taking a shower _____ thirty minutes.

10. My dad's been teaching English _____ he was 34 years old.

11. His aunt's been playing the guitar _____ two hours.

12. Her grandma has been taking a nap _____ 2:00P.M.

13. Amy has been doing the dishes _____ twenty minutes.

14. I've been driving _____ two hours.

15. She's been riding _____ thirty minutes.

16. It's been raining _____ one hour ago.

12-6-3 英文該怎麼說？

1.　How long have you been learning English?

我學英文已經學了 4 年了。

_____

2.　How long has he been riding the bike?

他已經騎腳踏車騎了 1 小時。

_____

3.　How long have your children been eating dinner?

他們從 1 小時前吃晚餐。

_____

4.　How long have your friends been studying Japanese?

他們從下午 3 點念日文。

5. How long have you been living here?

   從我是 3 歲 (three years old) 起住在這裡。

6. How long has your sister been playing the piano?

   她從一小時前彈鋼琴。

7. How long has your son been doing the dishes?

   他已經洗碗洗了 30 分鐘 (minutes) 了。

8. How long have you been reading the novel?

   我已經讀了 3 小時。

9. How long has he been taking a walk (散步)?

   他已經散步兩小時了。

10. How long have you been waiting for your girlfriend (女朋友)?

    我已經等 40 分鐘了。

12-6-4 改錯

1. I have been buying this car for three weeks.

2. She doesn't have seen you for a long time.

3. I have been living in Taichung since one year.

4. My mom learned computer for two months.

5. He has been done his homework for one hour.

6.   My dad has being talked to him for two hours.

7.   They have been waiting for her for one hour ago.

8.   We have been cooking for this afternoon.

9.   She has been take a nap for thirty minutes.

10.   My mom has been talking on the phone since an hour.

附錄

在《專門為中國人寫的英文課本》中級本的每一課中，我們都會介紹一個文法觀念或日常會話的常用句型，課文通常以短句或兩人對話的方式呈現。讀者學會每一課之後，可以參考附錄的範文，研究各種時態和文法規則如何在一篇文章中靈活運用。讀者讀過範文後，應該可以明瞭，即使只是一篇十來句的短文，因為句子所敘述事情的時間與口氣不同，時態也必須不斷的調整，不能只用一種時態（如現在式）。希望大家讀完附錄的三篇範文後，能對本書所介紹的文法觀念有一個通盤的瞭解與認識。

範文一

生字

often	常常
by	搭（交通工具）
ever	曾經
walk	走路（walk, walked, walked）
sometimes	有時
Friday	星期五
ill	生病（形容詞）
tell	告訴（tell, told, told）
rest	休息（rest, rested, rested）
stay	待在，留在（stay, stayed, stayed）
at home	在家
feel	感覺，覺得（feel, felt, felt）
Monday	星期一

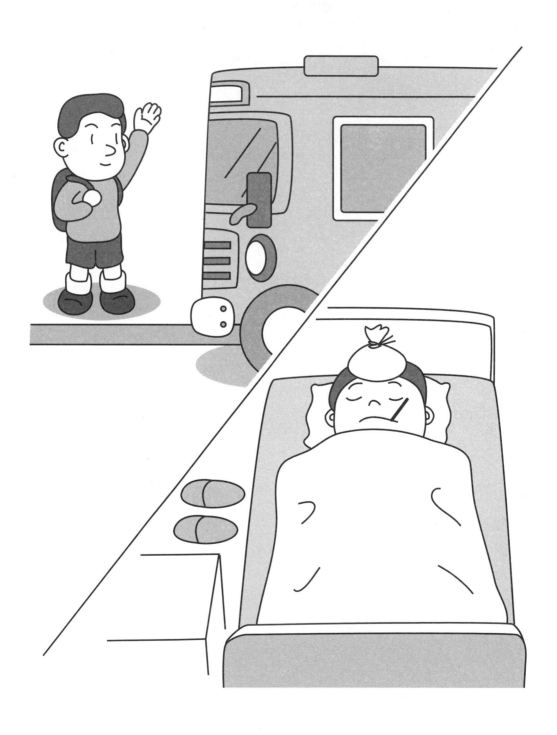

課文

John goes to school every day.[1] He often goes to school by bus.[2] Has he ever walked to school?[3] Sometimes he walks to school.[4] This Friday he didn't go to school.[5] He was ill.[6] His teacher called him.[7] She told him to rest.[8] He has been staying at home for three days.[9] Today he is feeling better.[10] Next Monday he will go to school.[11]

翻譯：

　　John 每天上學，他通常搭巴士上學。他曾經走路上學過嗎？有時候他會走路去上學。這星期五他沒有去上學，他生病了。他的老師打電話給他，她告訴他要休息。他已經待在家裡 3 天了，今天他覺得好一些，下星期一他會去學校。

課文解析

1. 上學是 John 每天例行做的事,動詞 go 用現在式, John 是第三人稱單數,動詞要加 s ,還記得 go 如果加 s 是 goes 嗎?

2. John 經常(often)搭巴士上學,這是 John 的習慣,用現在式來表示。

3. 問某人的經驗要用現在完成式(見第十一課),例如:
    Have you ever read that novel?(你讀過那本小說了嗎?)
    Have you ever been to China?(你曾經去過中國嗎?)

4. sometimes和often一樣,都在第十課出現過,用於一個人的習慣,通常用現在式來表示。

5. this Friday 已經過去了,說話的當兒可能是星期天(Sunday),所以用過去式。注意:過去式的否定句動詞前面要加助動詞 didn't ,且助動詞後面用動詞原形 go 。

6. ill 是形容詞,是不舒服,生病的意思。

7. 老師在 Friday 打電話給他,所以 call 得用過去式 called 。

8. him 是 told 的受詞。 tell 和 rest 兩個動詞之間不要忘了用 to 來連接。

9. 這是第十二課談到的現在完成進行式的用法。 How long has he been staying at home? He has been staying at home for three days.

10. John 目前身體的狀況不錯,用現在進行式。

11. next Monday 是下星期發生的事,動詞要用未來式 will go 。

範文二

生字

learn	學習（learn, learned, learned）
always	總是
sing	唱（sing, sang, sung）
song	歌
all together	總共
for	為了（介系詞）
happy	高興（形容詞）
happily	高興（副詞）
with	與，跟（介系詞）
together	一起

Amy has been learning English for three years.[1] She always likes to sing English songs.[2] Sometimes she sings songs with her friends.[3] How many English songs can they sing?[4] All together, they can sing thirty-five songs.[5] Yesterday they sang songs for John.[6] John was very happy.[7] He sang with them, too.[8] They sang happily together.[9]

翻譯

Amy 學英文已經 3 年了，她總是喜歡唱英文歌，有時她跟朋友一起唱歌。他們會唱幾首英文歌呢？他們一共會唱 35 首。昨天他們為 John 唱歌，John 非常高興，他也跟著他們唱，他們高興地一起唱著歌。

1. 這是第十二課教的現在完成進行式的用法。

   How long has Amy been learning English? She has been learning English for three years.

2. always(總是)在第十課出現過,用於一個人的習慣,通常用現在式來表示。like 後面的動詞可以是不定詞:I like to stay here.也可以是動名詞:I like staying here.

3. sometimes (有時)和 always(總是)在第十課出現過,用於一個人的習慣,通常用現在式來表示。

4. can 用來表示一個人的能力,是助動詞。問句時要把 can 放在主詞的前面,例如:

   Can you speak English?(你會說英文嗎?)

   Yes, I can.(是的,我會。)

   注意:助動詞後面的動詞用原形。 She can sing English songs.

5. song 是可數的名詞,複數後面要記得加 s。

6. 這句的語氣突然轉為昨天,動詞要轉換為過去式:sing → sang。

7. 與 6 一樣,be 動詞 is 要改為過去式 was。

8. 介系詞 with 後面要用人稱代名詞受格:they → them。

9. 形容動詞 sang 要用副詞:happy → happily。

範文三

 生字

pizza	披薩
a lot	非常
usually	通常
weekend	週末（不用上學、上班，通常從星期五晚上算起到星期天晚上為止）
a lot of	很多
piece	片、塊
eat	吃 (eat, ate, eaten)
decide	決定 (decide, decided, decided)
at home	在家
know	知道 (know, knew, known)

Mary likes to eat pizza a lot.[1] She usually eats two or three pieces of pizza.[2] Last weekend she ate a lot of pizza.[3] How much pizza did she eat?[4] She ate ten pieces of pizza.[5] On Monday morning she didn't feel good.[6] She decided to stay at home.[7] Now she is sleeping.[8] How long has she been sleeping?[9] I don't know.[10]

翻譯

Mary 非常喜歡吃披薩，她通常吃兩、三片披薩。上個週末她吃了很多披薩。她吃了多少披薩？她吃了 10 片披薩。星期一早上她覺得不舒服，她決定待在家裡。她現在正在睡覺。她已經睡多久了？我不知道。

課文解析

1. a lot 有 very much(非常)和 very often(常常)的意思，例如：
   I look a lot like my sister.(我看起來跟我的姊姊非常相像。)
   We go there a lot.(我們常常去那裡。)

2. she 是第三人稱，動詞要加 s。 usually 放在 she 和 eat 的中間，常使人忘了 eat 要加 s。 pizza 是不可數的名詞，複數不能加 s，需要用單位名詞 piece 來表達它的數量。

3. last weekend 要用過去式，記得 eat 的過去式是 ate 嗎？ a lot of 與 lots of 意思一樣。例如：
   There are a lot of people there.(那裡有很多人。)
   She made lots of money.(她賺了很多錢。)

4. pizza 不可數，用 How much 來問：How much pizza did you eat?
   piece 可以數，用 How many 來問：How many pieces of pizza did you eat?

5. one piece of pizza(一片披薩), two pieces of pizza(兩片披薩), three pieces of pizza(三片披薩)……。

6. 也許她吃得太多，肚子痛，所以覺得不太舒服(She didn't feel good.)休息一、兩天之後，她說不定會覺得比較好一點(She may feel better.)

7. decide 後面動詞接不定詞(to ＋動詞)：I decided to stay here.

8. now 是目前，描寫現在的狀況要用現在進行式: is sleeping。

9. 這是第十二課教的現在完成進行式：have(has)＋ been ＋動詞 ing。問句用 How long ＋ have (has)＋主詞＋ been ＋動詞 ing?

10. know 是動詞，現在式否定句時前面要加 don't。

總複習

I. 選擇題

1. (　　) A: Where did you find those two toy cars?

    B: I found (1) it (2) them (3) us in my grandma's bedroom.

2. (　　) I don't like my friend's computer game. I like (1) my (2) her (3) mine better.

3. (　　) Did your grandson write this novel (1) himself (2) hisself (3) himselves?

4. (　　) They live here by (1) themselve (2) themselves (3) theirselves.

5. (　　) The cat drank (1) a piece of (2) lot of (3) two bowls of milk today.

6. (　　) May I have two (1) glasses of water (2) glasses of waters (3) glass of water ?

7. (　　) Where can I find my (1) two hundreds (2) two hundred (3) two hundred of dollars?

8. (　　) I'd like (1) two piece of (2) two pieces (3) two pieces of pizza.

9. (　　) May I have (1) three scoops of ice creams (2) three scoops of ice cream (3) three scoops ice cream ?

10. (　　) I care about my parents' (1) healthy (2) healthily (3) health.

11. (　　) They live (1) happy (2) happily (3) happiness together.

12. (　　) I (1) were born (2) am born (3) was born in 1952.

13. (　　) I didn't know you (1) were (2) will (3) was younger than your

wife.

14. (　　) My cousin likes (1) read (2) reads (3) reading novels.

15. (　　) My grandma doesn't enjoy (1) cooks (2) cooking (3) to cook.

16. (　　) He stops (1) drinks (2) to drinks (3) drinking coffee.

17. (　　) He usually (1) goes (2) go (3) going to the library after lunch.

18. (　　) Have you (1) see (2) saw (3) seen that movie yet?

19. (　　) How long has he been (1) teach (2) taught (3) teaching Japanese?

20. (　　) I've been waiting for you (1) for an hour (2) since an hour (3) a hour ago.

II. 填充題

1. I read two novels yesterday. I love _____ a lot.

2. My students did it _____.(他們自己) I didn't help them.

3. A: Do you like your sister's bike or your bike better?

   B: I like mine, but she likes _____.(她自己的)

4. A: May I have some orange juice?

   B: It's on the table. Please help _____.

5. I don't have my _____ computer. I have to use my sister's.

6. I have had two _____(碗) of rice. I'm full(飽了).

7. May I talk to you for a _____ minutes(幾分鐘)?

8. I was born _____ 1978.

9. A: How _____ water do you need?

   B: Three bottles(瓶).

10. My uncle can never stop his _____(angry).

11. I'm crazy _____ this singer and her songs.

12. I decided _____ finish my homework tomorrow.
13. A: I _____ (很少) see you do the dishes.

    B: I hardly ever do them because that's my husband's job(工作).
14. I didn't know you _____ three years older than your wife.
15. A: Have you met?

    B: Yes. We _____ three years ago.
16. I haven't _____ the novel yet, but my brother read it two years

    ago.
17. How long has your sister been _____ (教書) in that school?
18. How many books has he _____?
19. Who _____ you been talking to?
20. I have been living in Taipei _____ I was a child.

III. 問答

1. Who gave your children so many comic books(漫畫書)？

   My grandparents _____.
2. How do you like those American novels?

   I like _____.(非常喜歡它們。)
3. Where did you and your sister put your bikes?

   I put _____(我的) in front of the house. She put _____(她

   的) behind the house.
4. Which cell phone do you like? Your sister's or yours?

   I like _____ better.(我的)
5. Did you make this cake?

   Yes, I _____. (我自己做的。)
6. Do you like your computer?

I don't like _____.

（我自己的電腦，我比較喜歡我哥哥的。）

7. May I help you?

Yes, I'd like _____.（兩球冰淇淋。）

8. How much rice did you eat for lunch?

I ate _____（3 碗飯）at noon.

9. How much fruit did you buy yesterday?

I _____.（買了一些芒果。）

10. How much money do you have?

I _____.（只有 35 元在口袋裡。）

11. Which year were you born in?

_____（依實際情況回答）

12. What do you care about?

I _____.（關心我自己的健康。）

13. What do you enjoy doing?

I enjoy_____.（與朋友一起唱歌。）

14. What did you decide to do on weekends（週末）？

We decided _____.（清掃我們的臥室。）

15. How often do you play the piano?

I _____.（我很少彈鋼琴。）

16. Does your granddaughter often play basketball?

No, _____.（她幾乎不打籃球。）

17. Have you been to China?

Yes, I have. _____（我去年去那裡的。）

18. Has your grandson started to learn English yet?

No, _____.（他還沒有。）

19. How long has it been raining?

It_____.（從昨天晚上開始下的。）

20. How long have you been waiting here?

We _____.（我們等了 30 分鐘了。）

IV. 改錯

1. I didn't give he's books to her.

2. They've finished the work by theirself.

3. This is himself room.

4. Who's cell phone is this? It's my friend's.

5. I just heard a good news.

6. She bought two breads this afternoon.

7. May I borrow three papers from you?

8. How many pizza did you eat tonight?

9. How much dollar do you have in your pocket?

10. We've been talking about his successful for hours.

11. He doesn't care about his healthy. He's been eating a lot of junk food（垃圾食物）.

12. I am decide to see her tonight.

13. He seldom finishes to do his homework.

14. I haven't readed his novels.

15. My aunt always works hardly.

16. I've given her some bread yesterday.

17. We've been knowing each other for many years.

18. She has just bought this new computer a week ago.

19. My English teacher has wrote many books.

20.   My grandma waited for me since an hour ago.

V. 英文該怎麼寫?

1.   這些芒果是他們的。

_____

2.   我的父母給了我們很多玩具車。

_____

3.   我不喜歡我的手機。我比較喜歡她的。

_____

4.   他沒有他自己的電腦。他用(use)我的。

_____

5.   我的兒子獨自一人做了一把椅子。我一點也沒有幫他忙(help him)。

_____

6.   誰泡了(made)一壺綠茶?

_____

7.   我的先生教 58 個學生。

_____

8.   你的祖父是哪一年出生的?

_____

9.   你的媽媽看起來比她妹妹年輕。

_____

10.   她是一位很幽默的老師。

_____

11.   你為什麼生氣的跟我說話? Why did you...

_____

12.   我決定自己一個人去看電影。 I decided...

13. 他今天下午開始讀這本小說。 He began...

14. 我的表哥通常下午會喝一杯咖啡。

15. 我總是喜歡到圖書館去讀英文(to study English)。

16. 好奇怪。她幾乎不鋪床,她先生鋪。

17. 她看過這部電影了嗎?

18. 我從小就住在台北。

19. 你信寫完了嗎?

20. 你從今天早上起就一直在寫信。

習題解答

第一課

1-3-1 填填人稱代名詞受格

1. them
2. it
3. her
4. us
5. him
6. you
7. her
8. him
9. them
10. them
11. it
12. them
13. it
14. it
15. them
16. it
17. it
18. it
19. it

20. it

1-3-2 英文該如何説

1. Yes, I like it
2. She gave me a bike.
3. Yes, she called me last night.
4. Yes, I can see her.
5. I saw him at school.
6. Yes, she likes them.
7. Yes, she gave us pencils.
8. I call it Spot.
9. Yes, he called us.
10. No, I don't like it
11. Yes, I can call you tonight.
12. Yes, I can. I play it every day.
13. Yes, I do. I read it every week.
14. I found them on the desk.
15. I like it
16. I play it
17. My parents called me this afternoon.
18. I found it in the park.

19. No, I didn't call her.

20. I read it last year.

第二課

2-3-1 選選看

1. (2)

2. (1)

3. (2)

4. (3)

5. (3)

6. (1)

7. (2)

8. (1)

9. (3)

10. (2)

2-3-2 英文該怎麼說

1. This cat is mine.

2. This desk is ours.

3. This cell phone is hers.

4. Those flowers are theirs.

5. This car is his.

6. These books are my English teacher's.

7. Those pencils are my parents'.

8. It is my brother's.

9. It is my friend's.

10. These cakes are ours.

2-3-3 用所有代名詞回答

1. hers

2. his

3. it isn't his

4. are not his（如果是女醫生則用 hers）

5. they're hers

6. they're not theirs

7. it isn't yours

8. it isn't hers

9. it isn't mine

10. they're not ours

第三課

3-3-1 填填看

1. his own

2. my own

3. her own

4. your own

5. their own

6. your own

7. our own

8. his own

9. her own

10. their own

3-3-2 將 -self 填進空格中

1. herself
2. themselves
3. ourselves
4. yourself
5. himself
6. himself
7. myself
8. yourselves
9. herself
10. ourselves

3-3-3 英文該如何說

1. She likes her own house.
2. My daughter bought it herself.
3. She makes the bed herself every morning.
4. She goes to school with her friends.
5. She plays it for herself.
6. It's my son's own car.
7. She has her own desk.
8. My daughter wrote it herself.
9. My son made it by himself.
10. She is talking to herself.

3-3-4 改錯

1. cooked → cook
2. hisself → himself
3. yourself → your own
4. yours → your
5. Do → Are
6. herself → her own
7. themself → themselves
8. was 去掉
9. ourself → ourselves
10. am 去掉

第四課

4-3-1 選選看

1. （3）
2. （1）
3. （3）
4. （1）
5. （2）
6. （3）
7. （1）
8. （2）
9. （3）
10.（1）

4-3-2 填填看

1. two pieces of

2. a pot of

3. a bowl of

4. a glass of

5. a cup of

6. a little bit of

7. a glass of, a cup of

8. some/ a little

9. three bags of

10. egg, two pieces of, a glass of

4-3-3 英文該怎麼説

1. There are two pieces of paper on Amy's desk.

2. He ate two bowls of rice for dinner.

3. My mom bought two loaves of bread this morning.

4. May I have a glass of orange juice, please?

5. A: Who made this pot of black tea? B: I made it myself.

6. I need some paper to do my homework.

7. I drink a cup of coffee every day.

8. There is a glass of water on the table.

9. I made three cups of tea.

10. Would you like something to eat?

4-3-4 改錯

1. glass → a glass

2. bowl → bowls

3. papers → paper

4. make → makes

5. red → black

6. coffees → coffee

7. a → any 或去掉

8. is → are

9. two → this（或 two glasses of）

10. bowl → bowls

第五課

5-3-1 數字的英文該怎麼説

1. thirty-two

2. eleven

3. eighty-seven

4. twelve

5. seventeen

6. seventy-nine

7. forty-six

8. twenty-five

9. five hundred

10. ninety-two

5-3-2 英文該如何説

1. This computer game is four hundred NT dollars.
2. There are eighty bags of rice in the house.
3. My grandma has eleven teapots.
4. All together, my students drank twenty bottles of Coke this afternoon.
5. My brother gave me eighteen books.
6. This desk is five hundred and ninety-nine NT dollars.
7. All together, his English teacher has twenty-three students.
8. There are sixty NT dollars in my mom's bag.
9. My sister makes nine hundred NT dollars a day.
10. The doctor read thirteen books this month.

5-3-3 加加看, 減減看
1. twelve
2. forty-one
3. eighteen
4. one hundred
5. twenty-three
6. sixty-eight
7. thirty
8. eighty-one
9. twenty-eight
10. ninety-four

第六課

6-3-1 算算看再填
1. five years younger
2. four months older
3. seven years younger
4. one year older
5. four years younger
6. three years younger
7. two years older
8. two years younger
9. four years older
10. two years younger

6-3-2 填填看
1. old
2. look
3. was, born
4. was, in
5. older than
6. were

7. years old

8. looks

9. about

10. look

6-3-3 改錯

1. are → is

2. old → older

3. You → Your

4. born → was born

5. at → in

6. are 去掉

7. You → Your

8. were → was

9. you → your

10. is look → looks

6-3-4 中文該如何說

1. How old is your grandma?

2. Her dog looks sad.

3. My cat looks older than your cat.

4. This book is older than that one.

5. His wife looks very young.

6. My grandpa was born in 1926.

7. His dad is ninety-three years old this year.

8. Which year was your husband born in?

9. Which dog is older?

10. He looks younger than eighty years old.

第七課

7-3-1 填填看

1. How many

2. How much

3. How much

4. How many

5. How much

6. How many

7. How much

8. How much

9. How many

10. How many

11. How much

12. How many

13. How many

14. How much

15. How many

7-3-2 看圖畫回答問題

1. There are three watermelons in the box.

2. I have twenty dollars in my pocket.

3. There is a bed in my sister's room.

4. I had two bowls of rice for dinner.

5. She bought two mangos and three apples.

6. They had six pieces of pizza for lunch.

7. I have a brother and a sister.

8. He ate four pieces of pork for dinner.

9. She just ate a scoop of ice cream.

10. It had two bowls of milk.

7-3-3 英文該如何回答

1. I drink eight glasses of water every day.

2. He would like to eat some pork.

3. Altogether, I have thirty-five books.

4. She only ate one bowl of rice.

5. I just ate three scoops of ice cream.

6. Altogether, they ate eleven pieces of watermelon.

7. I would like two mangos and three bananas.

8. I would like four pieces of pizza.

9. He only ate one scoop of ice cream.

10. I would like two pieces of chicken.

第八課

8-3-1 選選看

1. (2)
2. (1)
3. (2)
4. (3)
5. (2)
6. (3)
7. (3)
8. (1)
9. (2)
10. (2)
11. (2)
12. (1)
13. (2)
14. (3)
15. (1)
16. (1)
17. (2)
18. (1)
19. (2)
20. (3)

8-3-2 填填看

1. slowly
2. happily
3. happy
4. healthy
5. healthily
6. health
7. angry
8. angrily
9. anger
10. crazily
11. crazy
12. craziness
13. successful
14. success
15. successfully
16. successfully
17. lazy
18. laziness
19. slowly
20. slowly

8-3-3 改錯

1. healthy → health
2. health → healthily
3. successfully → successful
4. happy → happily
5. angrily → anger
6. healthy → health
7. angry → angrily
8. happy → happily
9. crazy → crazily
10. slow → slowly
11. crazy → crazily
12. anger → angry
13. happiness → happy
14. is care → cares
15. craze → crazy
16. healthy → health
17. slowly → slow
18. happiness → happy
19. crazy → am crazy
20. angry → angrily
21. am 去掉
22. Are → Do
23. craze → crazy
24. is make → makes（或 is making）
25. play → playing（或 She plays）

第九課

9-3-1 填填看

1. cooking
2. to read（或 reading）

3. doing

4. to play（或 playing）

5. to see

6. to see

7. to read（或 reading）

8. to play（或 playing）

9. looking

10. to study（或 studying）

11. learning

12. to learn

13. to drive

14. drinking

15. eating

9-3-2 改錯

1. making

2. go → to go

3. like to walking → like to walk（或 like walking）

4. to cook → cooking

5. like play → like to play（或 like playing）

6. making → to make

7. listen → listening

8. seeing → to see

9. go → to go

10. began to singing → began to

sing（或 began singing）

11. is keep → keeps

12. am → do

13. likes eat → likes to eat（或 likes eating）

14. like drink → like to drink（或 like drinking）

15. eating → to eat

9-3-3 英文該怎麼説

1. My brother hates to study math.

2. My mom began to read a novel.

3. Amy's cat likes to drink milk.

4. My friends like to have afternoon tea.（或 to drink）

5. My daughter began to play the piano today.

6. My cousins enjoy playing cards.

7. My dad hates driving to work.

8. He likes to eat rice.

9. David's dog enjoys taking a nap.

10. She likes to make cookies.

第十課

10-3-1（參考答案）

1. walk to school

2. go to see movies

3. drink milk

4. sleep late

5. listen to music

6. make the bed

7. get up before 8:00 A.M.

8. goes to bed late

9. reads novels

10. plays the piano

11. eats pork

12. dance happily

10-3-2 填填看

1. hardly ever

2. never

3. seldom

4. sometimes

5. usually

6. always

7. go to bed

8. gets up

9. never

10. sleep late

11. often

12. usually

13. strange

14. hardly ever

15. often

10-3-3 英文該怎麼說

1. He never eats breakfast.

2. My mom often calls my grandma.

3. His grandpa never sleeps late.

4. Amy's bird seldom drinks water.

5. My aunt often goes to Japan.

6. Her uncle always goes to Tainan by bus.

7. Do you always get up before seven?

8. My parents hardly ever eat pork.

9. Do you seldom drink Coke?

10. The usually eat ice cream after dinner.

第十一課

11-5-1 填填看

1. we have

We met one year ago.

did

We met at school.

2. Have

I'll read it tomorrow.

3. Has

has

did

went

4. Have

did

played

5. Have

learned

11-5-2 選選看

1. （3）

2. （2）

3. （3）

4. （3）

5. （1）

6. （2）

7. （2）

8. （3）

9. （2）

10. （1）

11-5-3 英文該如何説

1. She met the singer two years ago.

2. I haven't learned English yet.

3. My brother has taken a nap.

4. My sister has been to America.

5. My sister hasn't read this novel yet.

6. I'll ride the bicycle to school tomorrow.

7. My grandparents have never been to China.

8. He didn't play the piano today.

9. My cat hasn't drunk milk yet.

10. You dad has done the dishes.

11-5-4 改錯

1. Has → Have

2. do → done

3. have → has

4. goes → went

5. eat → eaten

6. played → play

7. buy → bought

8. wrote → written

9. hasn't → haven't

10. find → found

第十二課

12-6-1 填填看

1. eating

2. driving

3. playing

4. sleeping

5. reading

6. studying

7. taking

8. listening

9. taking

10. talking

11. writing

12. talking

13. teaching

14. doing

15. drinking

12-6-2 用 since 還是用 for

1. for

2. for

3. since

4. for

5. since

6. since

7. since

8. for

9. for

10. since

11. for

12. since

13. for

14. for

15. for

16. since

12-6-3 英文該怎麼說

1. I've been learning English for four years.

2. He's been riding the bike for an hour.

3. They've been eating dinner since an hour ago.

4. They've been studying Japanese since 3:00 P.M.

5. I've been living here since I was three years old.

6. She's been playing the piano since an hour ago.

7. He's been doing the dishes for thirty minutes.

8. I've been reading it for three hours.

9. He's been taking a walk for two hours.

10. I've been waiting for her for forty minutes.

12-6-4 改錯

1. have been buying → have bought

2. doesn't have → hasn't
3. since one year → since one year
   ago（或 for one year）
4. learned → has been learning
5. done → doing
6. being talked → been talking
7. ago 去掉（或 for → since）
8. for → since
9. take → taking
10. since an hour → for an hour（或
    since an hour ago）

總複習解答

I. 選擇題

1. （2）
2. （3）
3. （1）
4. （2）
5. （3）
6. （1）
7. （2）
8. （3）
9. （2）
10. （3）
11. （2）
12. （3）
13. （1）
14. （3）
15. （2）
16. （3）
17. （1）
18. （3）
19. （3）
20. （1）

II. 填充題

1. them
2. themselves
3. her own bike（或 hers）
4. yourself
5. own
6. bowls
7. few
8. in
9. much
10. anger
11. about
12. to
13. seldom
14. were
15. met
16. read
17. teaching
18. read
19. have
20. since

III. 問答

1. did
2. them a lot
3. mine, hers
4. mine
5. made it myself
6. mine. I like my brother's better
7. two scoops of ice cream
8. three bowls of rice
9. bought some mangos
10. only have thirty-five dollars in my pocket
11. I was born in（1986）.
12. care about my own health
13. singing with friends
14. to clean our bedrooms
15. seldom play the piano
16. she hardly ever plays basketball
17. I went there last year.
18. he hasn't
19. has been raining since last night
20. have been waiting for thirty minutes

IV. 改錯

1. he's → his
2. theirself → themselves
3. himself → his own
4. Who's → Whose
5. a good news → some good news
6. two breads → two loaves of bread
7. papers → pieces of paper
8. many pizza → much pizza（或many pieces of pizza）
9. much dollar → many dollars
10. successful → success
11. healthy → health
12. am decide →（have）decided
13. to do → doing（或把to do去掉）
14. readed → read
15. hardly → hard
16. I've given → I gave
17. been knowing → known
18. has 去掉
19. wrote → written
20. waited → has been waiting

V. 英文該怎麼寫？

1. These mangos are theirs.
2. My parents gave us many toy cars.
3. I don't like my cell phone. I like hers better.
4. He doesn't have his own computer.

He uses mine.

5. My son made the chair by himself. I didn't help him at all.

6. Who made a pot of green tea?

7. My husband teaches fifty-eight students.

8. In which year was your grandpa born?

9. Your mom looks younger than her sister.

10. She is a humorous teacher.

11. Why did you talk to me angrily?

12. I decided to go to the movie by myself.

13. He began to read this novel this afternoon.

14. My cousin usually drinks a cup of coffee in the afternoon.

15. I always like to study English in the library.

16. It's strange. She hardly ever makes the bed. Her husband makes the bed.

17. Has she seen the movie yet?

18. I've been living in Taipei since I was little.

19. Have you finished writing the letter yet?

20. You have been writing letters since this morning.

專門替中國人寫的英文課本　中級本（上冊）

2023年1月三版　　　　　　　　　　　　　　定價：新臺幣280元

著　　　者　文　庭　澍
策劃・審訂　李　家　同
叢書主編　何　采　嬪
校　　　對　林　慧　如
　　　　　　海　　　柏
　　　　　　Yvonne Yeh
封面設計　陳　泰　榮
插　　　圖　陳　玉　嵐

出　版　者　聯經出版事業股份有限公司
地　　　址　新北市汐止區大同路一段369號1樓
叢書主編電話　（02）86925588轉5305
台北聯經書房　台北市新生南路三段94號
電　　　話　（02）23620308
郵政劃撥帳戶第0100559-3號
郵撥電話　（02）23620308
印　刷　者　世和印製企業有限公司
總　經　銷　聯合發行股份有限公司
發　行　所　新北市新店區寶橋路235巷6弄6號2F
電　　　話　（02）29178022

副總編輯　陳　逸　華
總　編　輯　涂　豐　恩
總　經　理　陳　芝　宇
社　　　長　羅　國　俊
發　行　人　林　載　爵

行政院新聞局出版事業登記證局版臺業字第0130號

國家圖書館出版品預行編目資料

專門替中國人寫的英文課本 中級本 / 文庭澍著 .
李家同策劃 · 審訂 . 三版 . 新北市 . 聯經 . 2023.01
160 面 . 19×26 公分 .
ISBN 978-957-08-6767-1（上冊；平裝）
[2023年1月三版]

1.CST：英語 2.CST：讀本

805.18   112000581